Oscar de Mejo

JOURNEY TO BOC BOC

The Kidnapping of a Rock Star

HARPER & ROW, PUBLISHERS

To a little boy
from Rochester, New York—
MICHAEL

34850

Journey to Boc Boc: The Kidnapping of a Rock Star
Copyright © 1987 by Oscar de Mejo
Printed in the U.S.A. All rights reserved.

Library of Congress Cataloging-in-Publication Data
de Mejo, Oscar.
  Journey to Boc Boc.

  Summary: Charismatic rock star Jack Michaels is
so wonderful in his concerts and videos that extraterrestrial Lysidra kidnaps him to her planet and
attempts to win him away from his true love on Earth.
  [1. Extraterrestrial beings—Fiction. 2. Rock
music—Fiction. 3. Science fiction] I. Title.
PZ7.D3917Jo 1987   [E]   85-45261
ISBN 0-06-021579-8
ISBN 0-06-021580-1 (lib. bdg.)

Designed by Constance Fogler
1 2 3 4 5 6 7 8 9 10
First Edition

There was once a famous rock star named Jack Michaels. He was everybody's darling. When he sang, people sang with him. When he danced, they danced with him. He could just tap his foot or wave his hand and thousands would applaud.

Jack liked the applause, but when he wasn't onstage, he was a quiet fellow. He lived with his father, mother, sisters, and brothers in a big house.

Many girls were in love with Jack—movie stars, heiresses, beauty contest winners—all kinds of fans.

But Jack loved only Noona, a student at the Juilliard School of Music in New York. She was a bit shy, but she had a beautiful voice and she loved Jack with all her heart.

One night, when Jack was driving home from a rehearsal, he saw a strange girl waving from the side of the road. She looked so worried that he stopped. She didn't seem to recognize him, and she asked him, in a slightly foreign accent, to take her to the airport.

When they arrived, she said, "Put your car in the parking lot and walk with me to my flying saucer." Jack laughed. But she was pretty and mysterious, so he did as she said.

"What's that perfume you're wearing?" Jack asked. "This?" she asked, handing him her handkerchief. He sniffed it and passed out.

Jack woke up on another planet. He had been kidnapped! The girl who had kidnapped him turned out to be the daughter of the chief of planet Boc Boc. Her name was Lysidra. She had fallen in love with Jack when she saw him perform on interplanetary video.

"Please don't be angry with me," she said. "I had to do it. I wanted you to come give a concert here so much. I meant no harm."

The Boc Bocians were a nice bunch.

They all spoke English as well as Boc Boc, and they lived in round houses to keep from blowing away in the big winds.

They liked earthlings. Though their technology was far more advanced, they spent hours on end studying America, peering through clouds and darkness at our funny square homes, trillions of miles away, through machines that look like this.

They were crazy about music too. Lysidra took Jack to a fashionable discotheque to hear The Seven Mad Earthlings.

The band was playing a golden oldie called "My Old Boc Boc Home." Lysidra started humming along.

"They're very good," Jack said, relaxing. "But what are those peculiar instruments they're playing?"

That night, Jack dreamed of Noona. She was smiling at him sadly, and there were tears in her eyes.

Meanwhile, on Earth, the president of the United States called a press conference to announce the disappearance of the beloved Jack Michaels. The chief of police admitted there were no clues. The president blamed the Soviets, and the Soviets blamed the CIA.

The date was set for Jack Michaels' first performance on Boc Boc. The largest hall in town was chosen, with seats for fifty thousand fans. It was sold out. The sound of Jack's newly formed band was very weird. He was surprised himself, but he knew it was the most beautiful music he had ever made. The audience couldn't stop clapping.

Lysidra was sitting with her best friend, Sybil, in a box in the front row. "I'm in love with Jack," she whispered during the applause. "I love him, love him, love him!"

"Remember," Sybil warned. "He has a girlfriend on Earth."

"Yes, I know. He told me," Lysidra groaned. *"What shall I do?"*

At the party after the concert, Lysidra took Jack aside. "Try to forget Noona," she said. "I could make you happy here on Boc Boc. Don't you love me just a little?"

Jack shook his head sadly. "I'm sorry, Lysidra," he said. "You're a nice girl. And Boc Boc is a nice planet. But it's Noona I love."

Lysidra decided to see the wise old man of Lagosia.
"How can I make Jack love me?" she asked the sage.

"Lysidra dear," said the old man. "My advice to you is to fall in love with someone else. But if you must win Jack Michaels, bring Noona here."

"What?" cried Lysidra. "Bring her *here?*"

"Yes," said the wise one. "You must throw a party for the happy reunion of Jack and Noona—"

"No, no, never!" Lysidra covered her face and started to back away.

"At the party, introduce Noona to Albert the Magnificent."

Lysidra stared at the old man.

"Of course!" she yelled. "Why didn't *I* think of that?"

Albert the Magnificent lived in deserted Moon County. He had been living there for the past thirty years, ever since he had discovered that women couldn't resist him.

Doctors had studied Albert to find out why. Certainly it wasn't his looks. He was quite ugly. Nor was it his intelligence. He was rather stupid. Nor was it his charm. He was something of a bore. All they could come up with was that Albert had been born with some power, some kind of magnetic field that drew women to him.

So Albert, who didn't like women very much, and called himself a philosopher although he read only comic books, lived in an out-of-the-way land, seeing nobody except his Aunt Mimac.

He hardly ever went out by day, but took long strolls at night on the lonely heath.

Lysidra looked up Albert's file in her father's Bureau of Boc Boc Citizens and found his photograph.

"Ugh!" she said. "I can't imagine anyone falling for him." But he was her last hope.

On the night of the great party, Lysidra made a quick trip to Earth, where she kidnapped Noona and brought her safely back to Boc Boc. At midnight, an old-fashioned palanquin appeared in the ballroom, carried by four men wearing top hats. When the curtains were drawn apart, out stepped Noona.

"Oh, Jack!" she cried.

And they fell into each other's arms.

They were so happy to see each other that neither noticed a big, very fat woman in a long skirt come into the room. Lysidra quickly ushered her into a private chamber.

"Where is Albert the Magnificent?" Lysidra asked impatiently.

"He is tired from his journey," said Aunt Mimac. "The train was drafty, and he forgot his shawl. I hope he hasn't caught a cold."

Lysidra explained that Albert was to pass a test before being presented to Noona. Posing as a music professor looking for a secretary, he would interview three women. If they fell in love with him, he would be ready for the conquest of Noona.

"But he doesn't need a secretary," Aunt Mimac protested. "He has *me*!"

PHOTO SUNDIAL — BOCBOC

PHOTO DIAZ — BOCBOC

PHOTO ODILON   BOC BOC

Lysidra had handpicked the candidates herself. First, there was young Elouisa Mabelot. She was very lovely, but average in every other way.

Then there was Marteena Supson, who hated men. And finally, there was Sigurdine Maillard, who believed that love was the root of all evil.

Lysidra's best friend, Sybil, begged her not to go through with the plan.

"If you do something bad to someone, you're bound to get something bad in return," she warned.

But Lysidra just laughed.

Meanwhile, Miss Mabelot came to apply for the imaginary job.

"Oh, professor," she said. "Oh, professor!" And she leaped into Albert's arms.

Marteena Supson was the second to show up. As she stood in front of Albert, she turned pale. Then she began to sway. Finally, she fainted. As she fell she whispered, "Oh, what a beautiful sight!"

Last was Sigurdine Maillard. She sat down calmly and answered Albert's first question. Then she got up and asked to be excused, leaving her umbrella and purse on the chair.

In a moment, she came back carrying a big bouquet of roses.

"I have never known love," she said softly, kneeling in front of Albert. "But you may marry me anytime you like."

"Noona is doomed!" Lysidra cried triumphantly when she heard the news.

But Albert was worried. "I won't have to marry Noona, will I?" he asked.

"Oh, no," Lysidra assured him. "Just *act* as if you'll marry her until Jack thinks he's lost her forever. Then it's up to you."

Lysidra wasted no time inviting Noona to her home for tea. "I have a friend I'd like you to meet," she said. "A music professor. Perhaps during your stay on Boc Boc you'd like to take lessons from him. He's very learned."

"Ha ha," she chuckled to herself. "Lessons indeed!"

Noona was chatting pleasantly with Lysidra over jam and scones when a little man came into the room, bowed deeply to her, and lit a cigarette. He had three balls of hair on his head and a short, pointy beard. The conversation stopped.

"This is the great maestro I was telling you about—Albert the Magnificent," said Lysidra, watching Noona closely.

"How do you do," said Noona politely. She stifled a yawn and helped herself to another scone.

Lysidra began to fan herself violently with a napkin. Albert became fidgety.

"Lysidra," said Noona when Albert had gone, "there's something you should know. I really don't think Jack and I will be staying on Boc Boc much longer. You see, we're going to be married."

This time, it was Lysidra's turn to faint.

Albert the Magnificent couldn't believe he had failed. He decided to give it one more try. That night, he showed up at Noona's door with a bouquet of roses. "Ever since I first saw you..." he began, but she showed him to the door. "Thanks," she said, "but I'm in love with Jack."

It was Sybil who saw Noona and Jack off at the spaceport.

"Good-bye, good-bye," she called. "Don't forget Boc Boc. You're always welcome here."

She sighed as they lifted into the sky. "Poor Lysidra," she thought. "She'll be so unhappy. But it's for the best."

Jack and Noona had a splendid wedding on Earth. They decided to spend their honeymoon in New York. After all, they had already traveled rather far.

On their first morning as husband and wife, they opened the mailbox to find a postcard from Lysidra.

"Oh dear," said Jack, looking closer. For this is what he saw:

Dear Jack, I have married Albert. Yours truly, Lysidra